TRUE
Friendship
WITH
GIRLFRIENDS

LICIA JOHNSON

WESTBOW
PRESS®
A DIVISION OF THOMAS NELSON
& ZONDERVAN

Scriptures and additional materials quoted are from the Good News Bible © 1994 published by the Bible Societies/HarperCollins Publishers Ltd UK, Good News Bible© American Bible Society 1966, 1971, 1976, 1992. Used with permission.

This book is a work of non-fiction. Unless otherwise noted, the author and the publisher make no explicit guarantees as to the accuracy of the information contained in this book and in some cases, names of people and places have been altered to protect their privacy.

WestBow Press books may be ordered through booksellers or by contacting:

WestBow Press
A Division of Thomas Nelson & Zondervan
1663 Liberty Drive
Bloomington, IN 47403
www.westbowpress.com
1 (866) 928-1240

ISBN: 978-1-9736-1150-9 (sc)
ISBN: 978-1-9736-1151-6 (e)

Library of Congress Control Number: 2017919256

Print information available on the last page.

WestBow Press rev. date: 12/19/2017

Reflections

It was Kendra's first day of school at Columbia College, and she was excited. Tuesday was her Spanish II class. She thought to herself, *"Will I remember all the Spanish I learned my senior year?*

As the nine o'clock hour rolled around, more and more students hurriedly entered the class. Finally, along came Sarah, a Belizean with a perfect slim figure; a bright smile; and thick, gorgeous hair. Kendra whispered, "She's pretty, but I bet she's stuck up."

At the end of the semester, Kendra's judgment of Sarah turned out to be all wrong. Sarah was the friendliest young lady at the school. Why did Kendra go there, and why do many other women do the same?

This is a story about the friendship between two women, including the unexpected, the joys, and the ups and downs. How did these young ladies deal with their friendship as they reached adulthood? What is the best thing to do when you feel your friends are changing or are showing difficult new sides of their personalities?

Friendship—what is it, and what does it really mean to you? *Wikipedia* defines *friendship* as a "relationship of mutual affection between two or more people." Other characteristics include "mutual understanding and compassion; enjoyment of each other's company; trust; and the ability to be oneself, express one's feelings, and make mistakes without fear of judgment from the friend."

Let's look at Kendra, her friend Aubrie, and other young ladies to see how they handled their relationships and friendships. How did they unfold? Did they end happily?

Aubrie Murphy was born in St. Louis, Missouri, in 1981. She was an only child, and she had to be in control. Her parents spoiled her. She was born to be a leader, but sometimes she would get in her own way. She had a strong-willed personality, which made others take notice. Her parents, Georgia and Philip Murphy, were high school sweethearts and devout Catholics. Her father was biracial, white and Puerto Rican. Aubrie was a gorgeous baby with copper-brown skin and thick, curly black hair. She had a cute little mole between her eyes. People always asked her the same silly question: "Are you from India?" She never understood why people thought that.

Aubrie lived in a good home, was loved, and got all she needed and even more of what she wanted. When she was the tender age of five years old, her grandparents already had set up a $50,000 college fund. When Aubrie was nine years old, her mom told her several times, "Aubrie, things have changed. My job cut back on my hours, and your father's job cut his hours as well, so we can't spend money the way we used to."

"Mama, when will it get better?"

"Hopefully soon, honey. I really don't know."

Within a year and a half, Mrs. Murphy lost her job. They depended solely on her husband to take care of the family. During that time, it became a struggle for them to survive financially. Mr. Murphy heard that many families were moving north for better-paying jobs. New York, Chicago, and other cities had job markets that were off the charts. It was as if those with college degrees were celebrities. Companies were paying for families to move and also giving hefty bonuses. Mr. Murphy kept his eyes on everything happening in Chicago. He even started to read the *Chicago Tribune* newspaper to see if any opportunities opened up for him as an engineer.

One early Saturday morning in July, Mr. Murphy was watching the news. The broadcaster said, "If you are an experienced engineer, McCormick Place is looking to hire one hundred people. There will be a job fair from August 17 to August 22, from nine o'clock in the morning until two o'clock in the afternoon. Bring your résumés, and come prepared, because interviews will be conducted the same day."

"Wow!" exclaimed Philip. "Where is a pen? I've got to write this down. This is just what my family and I need to get back on our feet."

Mr. Murphy got busy updating his résumé and told his wife about the opportunity. "Georgia, guess what! I have great news."

"What, honey?"

"McCormick Place in Chicago is having a job fair for engineers, and I plan on going. They are paying big bucks too. What do you think?"

"That sounds great, honey. Maybe I can find a job as well. I've always dreamed of living in a big city. Now is the time for change."

Philip passed the engineer's test with flying colors and aced the interviewing process. Philip and Georgia Murphy prepared as best as they could for their trip to Chicago, and Georgia brought her long underwear, gloves, hat, earmuffs, and scarf.

Philip laughed. "Honey, what are you doing? It's not quite winter yet."

"Well, I heard about the hawk, and I don't like to be cold, so I gotta be ready, baby. You know me."

The Murphys looked at the Chicago papers for homes or apartments. They prayed for and believed in success. Georgia held the *Chicago Sun-Times* in her lap while she placed the *Chicago Tribune* on the coffee table. "Oh, help me, Lord, understand these prices! A two bedroom goes for four hundred fifty dollars a month? We can get more for our money in St. Louis for that amount." She stood up in frustration as the newspapers delicately fell to the golden shag rug.

Philip consoled her and caressed his wife. "Baby, don't worry. I believe deep down in my heart that God is going to bless us, and we will find favor in all that we need." He placed his clothes in the suitcase and closed it.

Aubrie walked into her parents' bedroom. "Mama, why are we moving? I don't want to make new friends all over again."

"Remember, Aubrie, our family is from the South, so we will come back to visit."

"Okay, Mom. You know it's hard for me to make friends. I'm shy."

"Yeah, I understand. You will be okay. God will get us through this adjustment period."

The drive was amazing. Aubrie hadn't realized how beautiful the hills and forest were. The Murphy family arrived in Chicago on a bright Saturday morning. It was a gusty day. People had to be careful; doors were flying open, and debris from the streets was dancing in yards and vacant lots. Mr. and Mrs. Murphy found a nice home to rent in the Hyde Park area. They chose William Ray Elementary School because parental involvement was high, and the Murphys wanted to know what was going on at all times in their daughter's school life. The neighborhood looked dead to Aubrie. She didn't remember seeing any schools or parks along the way. Aubrie only had the weekend to adjust to Chi-town because school started on Monday, September 7.

The First Day of School

"Aubrie, get up! I want you to be on time."

Fifteen minutes passed, and Georgia heard silence. She briskly walked to her daughter's room, and Aubrie was still sleeping. Georgia flicked on the light. "Aubrie, get up! Don't have me pull you out of bed! I don't have time this morning. I've gotta drop you off and then be on my way to the new job, and I definitely don't want to be late."

"Okay, okay, Mom," whispered Aubrie. "I'm getting up, but I don't want to go. I don't know anybody!"

"It takes time, Aubrie. First days are sometimes bumpy. You'll be fine," said Georgia.

Aubrie finally got herself together. She dressed in her favorite color: pink. Her corduroy skirt went well with her multicolored sweater and tights.

Georgia could see the anxiety in her daughter's face and eyes. "Aubrie," she said as she pulled her daughter close to her, "remember, this is the day the Lord has made. Let us rejoice and be glad, okay? Everything is going to be all right. Give me a hug, and eat your breakfast."

"Okay, Mom, thanks," Aubrie said. Then she whispered to herself, "Aubrie, rejoice and be glad!"

As mother and daughter hurried to the car, Aubrie noticed another little girl her age down the street. She watched quietly and thought, *I wonder if she goes to my school.*

As Mom and Aubrie were driving in the car, they passed a little red vehicle. Aubrie watched to see if the car followed them.

"Aubrie, you okay?" her mom asked.

"Yeah, just thinking." Aubrie turned around for a second time, and she spotted the car with the familiar girl in it. She whispered to herself, "They look like a nice family, so she has to be nice too."

"Aubrie, what are you doing?"

"Oh, nothing. I'm looking at the environment and my surroundings."

"Well, make sure you do the same today in class.

"Okay, Mom." She saw the other children laughing, playing, and talking. "They look so happy. I hope I make a friend today or this week. Where is that other girl I saw?"

"Aubrie, give me a kiss, and pay attention in class. You hear?

"Yes, Mom." She grabbed her purple-and-pink book bag and her Wonder Woman lunch box and purse. "Bye, Mom. See you later."

"Okay, sweetie, be good!"

Aubrie got out of the car and closed the door, and she dropped all her stuff. "Man, what a great day I'm having."

Kendra walked up. Kendra Sands was an African American with a smooth dark brown complexion and bright brown eyes, and she loved to talk. She had been born in Chicago in 1980 to Mr. Earl and Mrs. Melodia Sands. She was also an only child. Kendra had always dreamed of being a big sister, but it was a struggle for her mom to get pregnant. Her parents had been blessed with Kendra's birth and decided not to have any more children. Kendra found every opportunity to make a new friend. She had a passive personality, letting things slide. She always avoided confrontation and was seen as a compromiser, always giving others the benefit of the doubt.

"Hello. Do you need some help?" Kendra said.

"Um, yeah, sure, thanks."

"I'm Kendra. What's your name?"

"I'm Aubrie."

"Cool," said Kendra. "You have a nice name. Here you go. Are you new? I've never seen you before."

"Yeah, I'm from St. Louis, and I've only been here since this weekend."

"Wow, Aubrie, I love your hair. Is it real? I would love to have hair like that."

Aubrie responded, "Yeah, it's real, and thank you. My daddy is Puerto Rican. I think that's where I get my curly hair from. People tell me I look like Jennifer Lopez. What do you think?"

"Really? Maybe a little. So, Aubrie, how do you like Chicago thus far?"

"It's okay. A little chilly. But I haven't had a chance to do much."

"Let's go inside," said Kendra.

"Okay."

"By the way, what grade are you in?"

Aubrie responded, "Fourth."

"Wow, me too," said Kendra. "Aubrie, we should have fun this year. Ms. Stocks is the best teacher I ever had. She's nice and fair, and we learn so much. She taught social studies last year and made learning exciting!"

As the girls walked together, they decided to sit next to each other in the middle of the class. Aubrie placed her book bag on her desk and pulled out her notebook. She grabbed her pen and began to write.

Kendra took notice and said, "Wow, I like the way you write. You think you can teach me how to write my name like you do?"

"Sure, no problem."

Bruno, a fellow classmate, saw them and noticed Aubrie immediately. "Hey, Kendra, what's up? Who is your new friend?"

"Bruno, this is Aubrie, and she is from St. Louis."

"Hello, Bruno," Aubrie said.

"Hello, Aubrie. It's nice to meet you, and I love your hair. The longer I look at you, the more you remind me of Jennifer Lopez."

"Thanks, Bruno."

Aubrie's first day of school was nice. She thought about what her mom had said and it was true. She thought, *Regardless of what happens, I will rejoice in the Lord. I met a new helpful friend in Kendra.*

Over the next six months, Kendra and Aubrie became good friends. They talked several times on the phone during the week. It was the start of a beautiful friendship. They appeared to have an instant connection; it was almost as if they were sisters. One reason Aubrie liked Kendra so much was because she had qualities Aubrie longed for. She was outgoing and not shy to voice her opinion. She was a confident young lady in control of her destiny and definitely a leader, not a follower. She had a strong personality.

After a long day at school, Aubrie arrived at home and did her homework immediately so she could call Kendra. Kendra was popular with all the boys. She always had the 411 on everything, and Aubrie wanted to know it.

The phone rang at three o'clock. "Who could this be? Hello?" Aubrie said.

"Hey, Aubrie. Girl, what's up?" Kendra said.

"Nothing. I'm doing my homework."

"What subject?"

"English."

Kendra responded, "Oh, do you have a lot to do?"

"Yes, but I can chat quickly. What are you up to, Kendra ?"

"Nothing. I called to tell you about that cute new boy, Corey. Girl, he kept smiling at you. Did you not feel it?"

"I guess not, Kendra. When was this?"

"When you raised your hand to answer that math question Mrs. Kendell asked."

"Oh, really?"

"Yeah. Aubrie, I think he really likes you."

"Well, he is kind of cute," said Aubrie lightly. "Kendra, hold on. I think I hear my mother coming. Girl, I gotta go. If my mom sees me on the phone, I'll get in trouble. I will call you later tonight."

"Aubrie, please remember to call me back. I've got some juicy information for you."

"Don't worry. I will."

***

The next day, Kendra saw Aubrie down the block, walking to school. Kendra yelled, "Aubrie! Hey, girl, what happened?"

"What do you mean, Kendra ?"

"You were supposed to call me back."

"Oh, girl, I forgot. I'm sorry. We can talk tonight."

"Aubrie, I thought you were better than that. I really wanted to talk last night."

"Man, I said I was sorry. You are so sensitive. Can you please remember to call me on Fridays and the weekend?"

"Why?" said Kendra.

"Because my mom caught me hanging up the phone, and my mama don't play. Do you think you can remember that?"

"Yeah, sure, relax, girl. Everything is going to be all right." Aubrie responded, "It better be."

The bowling season was nearing, and Kendra was interested in getting involved in the league. The ladies entered the bowling alley doors together. "Aubrie, I invited Makayla, so she will be joining us," Kendra said.

"Okay."

Twenty minutes later, along came Makayla. She had a light complexion and nice brown eyes. Her bubbly personality and laughter were contagious, and she had a chunky frame and short sandy-brown hair. All the other girls excluded Makayla, but Kendra made sure she included her. Kendra truly enjoyed her company, and she noticed how strong Makayla was. Makayla did not allow the other girls to upset her. She did her best to ignore them, and when that didn't work, she attacked them with her words.

"Hey, Makayla. How are you? And what took you so long?" said Kendra.

"Girl, Sophie was at it again, trying to fight me."

Sophie was the beautiful snob in class. She was smart and had long, silky dark brown hair. She had a clique of others following her every move, and all the boys were after her.

"For real?" Kendra said.

"Yeah. I told her, 'Girl, I don't have time for your foolishness,' and I ran, 'cuz you know she's too cute to sweat."

"Ha, yeah, girl, I know. I don't care for her at all," said Kendra.

"Hey, ladies, I'm ready to bowl. Why are we standing around talking?" Aubrie said.

"Okay, Aubrie, relax. We are coming," said Kendra.

As the ladies settled at lanes one and two, Aubrie said, "I really don't know how to bowl, so will you guys help me?"

"Sure," replied Kendra. "Aubrie, you will be fine. Plus, it's a game, and it is supposed to be fun. I hope you are not a sore loser."

Aubrie frowned and rolled her eyes at Kendra.

"Aubrie, what do you like to do for fun? If we do well bowling today, we can join the league here. I am so excited about bowling. This is great," said Kendra.

"I like shopping for clothes and putting outfits together."

"Okay. Hey, Aubrie, they have a bowling league on Fridays for the youth. We should join. What do you think?" Kendra decided to join and asked Aubrie to be a teammate. Kendra had skills, as she came from a bowling family. Her grandmother, mother, father, brothers, uncles, aunts, and cousins bowled, so it was easy for Kendra to score 100.

Aubrie had a competitive spirit and did not like to lose at anything. At one time, Kendra bowled a 125, and Aubrie's score was 45. Aubrie was not good, and little did Kendra know, it affected her self-esteem. Makayla and Kendra were having a ball, laughing at each other and gossiping about the other kids at school. However, Aubrie was not a good bowler and felt left out. While Makayla was bowling, Aubrie brought Kendra to the side and said, "I don't like her. Why did you invite her?"

Kendra, shocked, said, "I can't believe you. You gotta get to know her. She is so much fun."

As they finished whispering, Makayla asked them, "What's wrong? Is everything okay?"

Aubrie answered, "I have more fun when you are not around. Isn't that right, Kendra?"

"Oh no! That is not true. Girl, you are one of my very good friends. Don't let crazy Aubrie lead you into her own little world."

"That's okay," said Makayla. "I understand. This is my last game. See you later, Kendra." Makayla gave Aubrie an up-and-down look as if to say, "You are not worth speaking to," and rolled her eyes.

Kendra waved goodbye, sighed, and rolled her eyes at Aubrie. Aubrie responded, "Now we can have fun, just you and me."

"I don't think so. You have ruined this day. I will talk to you later."

"What? Why? What did I do?"

"You are so selfish. You could have at least kept those comments to yourself."

"Hey, Kendra, are we still teammates?"

Kendra continued walking away, waving her hand, as if she didn't care anymore. That incident was an early sign of Aubrie and her controlling ways, but Kendra did not take note.

Aubrie was a control freak and had an assertive personality. She had to make all decisions, including where and when they would go—everything. Aubrie appreciated one-on-one friendships where no one else interfered. That was how she liked it. Aubrie and Kendra hung out all the time and talked on the phone almost every day. Every time Aubrie called Kendra to hang out, Kendra never said no. Kendra continued to be a yes-person to Aubrie, even as they became adults.

Melodia Sands, Kendra's mother, thought this was dangerous behavior. Melodia wanted to know how Kendra was doing in school, so she decided to open a conversation in the kitchen as she prepared breakfast. "Hey, baby girl! What's going on? What have you been up to?"

"Oh, not much. I made a new friend this year. Her name is Aubrie. She's from St. Louis, and I'm doing my best to help her adapt. Aubrie, Makayla, and I went bowling yesterday."

"How did that go?"

"It was okay. I really enjoy hanging out with them."

"That's good, but who is the one you are always on the phone with?"

"Oh, that's Aubrie."

"Hmm, I'm not so sure about that young lady. You be careful. I sense something not nice about this Aubrie."

"She's cool. Don't worry."

For the next couple of weeks, the girls' friendship became tighter, as if they were blood related. Melodia already had a bad feeling about Aubrie, and she did her best to hold her peace. When Melodia walked in the door from work one evening, Kendra was on the phone again with Aubrie.

"Is this a daily ritual?" Melodia said.

"Mom, are you talking to me?" whispered Kendra.

Melodia frowned and waved her hand as if to say, "Don't worry about it."

Kendra knew when her mother was upset, so she decided to end the conversation with Aubrie. "Girl, I gotta go."

"Why?" said Aubrie. "Is your mom making you get off the phone?"

"No, Aubrie, I've been on long enough. I'll talk to you tomorrow."

"Okay, Kendra., Bye."

"Bye."

"Every time I come home, you are on the phone. Was that Aubrie?" Melodia said.

"Yes, Mom. Everything is fine!"

"Yeah, okay, but can you not be on the phone when I come home? Can you go to her house? Where does she live?"

"Oh, she lives within walking distance."

"See? Perfect. Why don't you visit her tomorrow instead of running up my phone bill?"

"Okay, Mom, will do," Kendra said, smiling. "You know what, Mom? I think Aubrie and I will be friends forever!"

"Are you sure about that? Forever is a long time."

"Mom, why are you so skeptical? It can happen."

"I know, baby girl, but things can change, and so do people. You may not want to listen to me now, but down the road, you are going to say I was right. I know you enjoy Aubrie's company, but you should also have other friends. It's almost as if Aubrie is your only friend. That's not healthy. What if something happens to her? What would you do?"

"Oh, Mom, you are overreacting. I have other friends, like Makayla, but Aubrie is my best friend. That's why we spend so much time together."

"Okay, okay, I understand that. I actually like Makayla better than Aubrie. But you have to make your own decisions and learn from them. Please think about what I am saying. Have fun."

"Yes, Mother," she responded playfully.

Notice Negative Tendencies

The girls grew closer and closer as their eighth-grade graduation approached. Even though they planned on attending different high schools, they remained tight and spoke on the phone every other day. They felt they didn't need any other friends. It was as if they had their own little club. The girls clung to one another. Their friendship was built on trust and dependability. Both girls had secrets and shared them with each other.

They were the best of friends, and they always had each other's back when it came to hanging out. Whether going to the corner store for snacks or to Marshall Field's for the latest styles, jeans, and makeup, they were there. Aubrie went to a fashion design school, and Kendra studied liberal arts to prepare for a singing career. After the summer and the new school year, the girls continued hanging out at the mall and being typical teenagers.

Their senior year in high school, they were inseparable. They declared that they were best friends and would be for a lifetime.

As their senior prom approached, the girls were excited about shopping for their gowns and choosing brand-new hairstyles. Since Aubrie was at the hair salon 24-7 and worked there as a part-time shampoo girl, she knew exactly what she wanted. Shakira, the owner of Glamorous Hair Kuts, was well known for her sophisticated cuts and hair designs. After Kendra saw Aubrie's hair, she also wanted Shakira to give her the hookup for her prom style too. Aubrie and Kendra decided to visit each other's house to take pictures before heading to the special event.

In the late '80s and '90s, more teens were having premarital sex, and that was the topic of discussion after prom was over. "Hey, Kendra, how are you, and what time did you make it in last night?" Aubrie asked.

"Oh, Van brought me home around midnight. How about you?"

"Girl, we went to breakfast at Denny's, and I didn't get home until three in the morning."

"Wow, your parents were okay with that?"

"Yep. So, Kendra, did you guys do anything afterward? Breakfast, hotel, motel, Holiday Inn?"

"Girl, no. We did a horse-and-carriage ride. It was cold but nice, intimate, and romantic. It was fun."

"Oh, okay, if you say so."

"Van mentioned a hotel once or twice, and I was like 'No! I'm not interested. Take me home.' But I did surprise him with a kiss after he walked me to my door."

"Really, Kendra? How was it? Can he kiss?"

"He's okay."

"Kendra, it sounds like you had a good time with Van."

"Yeah, we did. Well, I gotta go. Talk to you tomorrow, Aubrie."

"Okay, bye."

Aubrie owned a car, so the ladies were able to go shopping almost every weekend. For some reason, Kendra continued to go shopping with her even if she didn't feel like it. She felt obligated to do so.

Kendra called to see what Aubrie was up to. "Hey, Aubrie, how are you, and what's goin' on?"

"Oh, nothing, Kendra. What's up with you?"

"I want to buy a new purse, and I would like for you to help me shop for one."

"Well, do you have a price range, and where do you want to go? The mall or Marshall Field's?"

"I know you don't care for JCPenney, but that's where I want to go."

"Hmm," Aubrie said. "So, Kendra, when do you want to go?"

"Aubrie, how about we go today? Since it is Saturday, they should have some good sales. Let's go to Ford City."

"Okay, I will pick you up at two o'clock."

"Cool, see you then."

Hours later, Kendra heard the sound of birds singing; it was her new ringtone. She picked up her phone and saw that it was Aubrie.

"Hey, Kendra, I'm outside," Aubrie said.

"Okay, I'm coming out."

Kendra walked to the car, smiling and waving. Aubrie smiled, but she turned it off quickly as if she really didn't feel like smiling. Why did that bother Kendra? She never brought it up in discussion. Kendra opened the door, sat comfortably, and reached for her seat belt, and Aubrie pulled off, headed to the mall.

"Hey, Kendra, what does that button say on your jacket?"

"It says, 'I Love Jesus.' Do you like it? I can get you one."

"Oh, where did you get that from?"

"My dad gave it to me."

"What made you decide to wear it today?"

"My dad put it on my jacket, and I decided to keep it there. What's wrong? You don't like it? Does it make you feel uncomfortable?"

"No," answered Aubrie. "I was wondering if it was your choice or if your father told you to wear it."

"I don't see what the problem is. If someone you love gives you a gift, wouldn't you display it or wear it?"

"Never mind. Let's drop it," Aubrie said with an attitude.

"Fine," responded Kendra. Kendra thought to herself, *What was that all about? We are both believers. How come she appears to not agree with me?*

"So, Kendra, what kind of purse are you looking for?" Aubrie asked.

"Um, I want something different, but I'll just go with black. I don't know. I will figure it out when I get there."

"Okay."

Kendra bought her new purse and continued to shop and walk throughout the mall. All of a sudden, Aubrie became suspicious and was no longer walking with Kendra. She started walking away behind her, as if she were stalking her. It felt uncomfortable for Kendra, and when she turned around to look for Aubrie, Aubrie was blocks away and had the strangest look on her face.

"Aubrie, what are you doing? Can you try to keep up and walk with me?"

"Okay. It's okay. I'm here."

Kendra felt uneasy and frowned. *What's wrong with her? I just don't get it. Lord, what's going on? Is she tripping because I'm taking control? Is she having a hard time following me?* Kendra pushed that weird event to the side and continued to shop. "Let's go to Bath and Body Works. I need some new fragrances."

Aubrie always had something negative to say about the things Kendra liked, such as Bath and Body Works products. "I don't like that. Who wants to smell like sweet fruit and everybody else in the world?"

"But, Aubrie, the sweet pea scent is their best seller. Smell it. Can you truly be honest and say that doesn't smell good?"

"Girl, it's okay, but what's a sweet pea?"

"Yeah, I guess you're right, but I still like the way it smells." Kendra agreed with Aubrie because she felt friends had to have the same interests.

Aubrie had a regulating spirit, as if she thought she were Kendra's big sister or mother, even though Kendra was about one year older than Aubrie. Aubrie was vocal on everything Kendra did. For example, she always judged Kendra regarding what she should do or buy. Kendra had sinus issues and needed a humidifier. She'd gone to the store and bought what she could afford, which was a child-friendly design, an elephant. At the time, that was what she'd needed, and it was for her bedroom. When that conversation had come up on the phone, it was a problem for Aubrie.

"Yeah, Aubrie, with the weather changing, I had to buy a humidifier for my room. It definitely makes a difference, and I feel so much better."

"Where did you get it from, and how much was it?"

"I went to Bed, Bath, and Beyond, and it was thirty-five dollars."

"Thirty-five dollars? What kind of humidifier is that?" said Aubrie.

"It's for children—an elephant. It's kind of cute."

"Girl, why did you buy that? It's for children."

"So? It's still a humidifier, and the price was right for me. Don't worry. I can always upgrade later."

Aubrie responded, "Hmm, all I can do is shake my head."

Kendra said, "Yep, that's all you need to do. I will talk to you later," and she hung up the phone. Why was Kendra following her every move? Kendra would take in her criticism and not buy certain products because of Aubrie's comments. Wasn't that crazy? But she later realized she needed to buy things she liked.

The following week, the ladies went shopping again to hang out.

"Aubrie, let's go to the record store so I can look for some new music. I gotta learn a variety of songs so I can go to the Apollo in New York! I wanna be a star so bad I can taste it."

"Yeah, okay, Kendra, let's go."

As they entered the store, Anita Baker's "Giving You the Best That I Got" was blaring. "Oh, I love this song," Kendra said, and she began to sing loudly enough that Aubrie could hear her.

"Kendra, please, let Anita do the singing. You are messing up the song."

"What?"

"Kendra, I'm just playing. Relax. You take things too seriously. Go ahead; keep singing. I won't say a word!" Aubrie continued smiling and giggling to herself.

"That's okay, Aubrie. I don't like to be criticized. I will keep quiet, but you know what? I think you are jealous!"

"Jealous of what?"

"My singing ability. You wish you could sing like me, but you are horrible—that's why you mess with me all the time. But that's okay; you do you, and I'm gonna do me. The Lord showed me a revelation about my future with singing, and I just might appear on *The Oprah Winfrey Show* real soon."

Aubrie looked dumbfounded and could not believe her ears. "Hmm," responded Aubrie as she silently rolled her eyes at Kendra.

Kendra caught herself. She could not believe she'd just said that. Kendra took a deep breath and softly hummed the song to herself. The more time Kendra spent with Aubrie, the more she noticed Aubrie's negative tendencies. Kendra usually kept quiet to avoid confrontation, but she could no longer hold her tongue. Even though Kendra noticed Aubrie's conflicting negative attitudes, Kendra remained loyal as her friend; she wasn't ready to let go yet.

The girls graduated from high school, and they planned on making that summer the best. At the Puerto Rican Fest, Aubrie and Kendra hung out. Kendra had a new hairdo and was dolled up to the max, being natural and loving it. Kendra was cool, joyful, and friendly, talking to strangers, as her mother usually did. She was enjoying herself while hanging out with her mom and her girlfriend. Then she caught Aubrie's face. It was bent all out of shape like a car in a head-on collision. Kendra said to herself, *What is wrong with her? I'm gonna act like I don't even see it. Because if I acknowledge or question it, she will deny it anyway. Oh well. Did I do something wrong? Nope, I doubt it.* It was not the first time Kendra had noticed Aubrie showing anger. *Sometimes I think she doesn't even realize that discomfort is written all over her face. I don't know what's going on, but her attitude is starting to get on my nerves.*

As Kendra continued to walk with the Lord, she became brand new and then some. Most described her as a sweet spirit and a fabulous personality. People loved talking to her and being around her. That infuriated Aubrie, and she didn't understand it. It appeared to make matters worse in their friendship. When they were girls, their friendship was based on honesty. They both advised each other on the issues of life and tried to make life easier. However, as time rolled on and they approached adulthood, Kendra was not confrontational. She thought it would be best to tell Aubrie what she wanted to hear, and that just made matters worse between them. The ladies were going in separate directions regarding the friendship.

Kendra was a silly soul and carefree, which seemed to make Aubrie start to dislike her even more. As both ladies continued to hold on to their shoestring friendship, Aubrie invited Kendra to Women's Workout World. Kendra realized that Aubrie had low self-esteem and thought she was fat, while in actuality, she was a thin young lady. She was obsessed with losing weight, staying healthy, and working out.

Aubrie called Kendra and said, "Hey, Kendra, what's going on?"

"Nothing. Just watching TV. What's up?"

"Well, you know I am trying to maintain my weight, and I've joined Women's Workout World. We should plan on going together. You know we are not getting any younger!"

"Yeah, I know. So when do you want to go, Aubrie?"

"How about next Saturday morning?"

"Okay, see you next Saturday. Bye."

They arrived at ten o'clock in the morning. Aubrie was ecstatic, grinning from ear to ear. Kendra was just being her regular bubbly self. Susie, a short and chunky lady, greeted them at the door. "Hey, Aubrie, how are you?"

"Good. This is my friend I told you about, Kendra."

"Hey, Kendra, welcome. I will give you a tour first, and then you can do your workout after."

"Okay," said Kendra.

As Kendra finished the tour, Aubrie joyfully rushed to her side. "What do you think? You think you will join?"

"I don't know, Aubrie. I don't think my budget will allow it."

Aubrie said, "Your budget?"

"Yeah, girl. I am really trying to watch my finances, and right now it's probably best that I just do my own workouts for free. That's what I was telling Susie, and she understood me."

Aubrie frowned and said, "Maybe you can do it on a trial basis."

"Naw, Aubrie, I've got to let this one go for now."

"Kendra, you only live once, so enjoy it by getting into shape. It will be fun!"

"Aubrie, that sounds great, but I don't need to spend money I don't have. I can revisit this at a later date if need be. Plus, I can exercise at home. What a great way to save money!"

As Susie approached Kendra and began to talk, Aubrie stepped back with an attitude. Kendra noticed it but didn't say anything. What could she say? And if she did, Aubrie would deny the entire situation. Kendra was not sure what was going on. Was Aubrie angry that Kendra was money conscious or cheap? Or did she think that every time they hung out, Kendra rejected her ideas?

September was right around the corner, and Aubrie would be attending Roosevelt University. She'd changed her mind about fashion and would be studying African American studies.

One of her dreams was to meet her husband in college, but if she didn't, that was okay too because she had to stay focused on her studies.

***

For three years, the ladies did their thing in college, and they really didn't have time to chat, not even during the summer breaks. That was when the friendship started changing for the worse.

Kendra reflected while writing in her journal:

> How the years have sped by! And I never thought my friendship with Aubrie would be what it is today. We only girl-talk once or twice a month compared to speaking several times a week when we were teenagers. What happened? Did we grow apart? Was it always there, and one day it just hit? Boom! I never thought it would be like this, but times change, and people do too. More importantly, things happen that cause people to show their true colors. Change is inevitable. It's going to happen whether we like it or not.

Something else that separated the ladies was their attitude toward animals. Kendra loved all animals, and Aubrie hated them. The ladies enjoyed walking to exercise but also to talk about life. If Kendra saw a squirrel running up a tree, she would use her funny baby-talk voice to try to communicate with the squirrel. "Aw, Aubrie, look at the cute little squirrel. It's so precious!"

Aubrie would respond by looking at Kendra with disgust, silently shaking her head.

The Shift Takes Place: Aubrie Meets Tyson

God will shift the situation, and more importantly, he will open our eyes, hearts, and minds.

It was a beautiful autumn Monday morning, October 20, 1993. It was nine o'clock, and Aubrie was running late for her African American history class. She had always enjoyed researching different cultures. She rushed down the hall, searching for room 308. As she studied each room number, she noticed a handsome guy who appeared to be lost. Suddenly, he found his way and disappeared. Aubrie said to herself, "Maybe that's my class. Let's see." Walking slowly, she approached the area and looked at the door: African American History. "Oh, this is my class. Cool." She went into the room and searched for a seat near the window.

Mrs. Bob said, "Thank you for joining us, young lady."

Aubrie nervously smiled quietly. She inspected the room to see if she knew anybody, and there he was, the handsome guy. He was the model type—tall, built, and a chocolate delight! He stared at her, nodding to say hello. She tipped her head his way and began to sweat and grow warm on the inside. She said to herself, *Girl, relax. This is the first encounter. Don't get too excited. Wait to see if anything develops.*

After an hour of lecture, she was tired and needed a break, and so she headed to the café lounge for a drink.

"Excuse me. Hello," said the young man.

"Oh, are you talking to me?" said Aubrie.

"Yes. I'm Tyson Williams. Nice to meet you."

"I'm Aubrie Murphy. Nice to meet you too."

"So where are you headed, Aubrie?"

"I'm thirsty. Gotta take a break."

Tyson said, "Can I join you?"

"Sure, that would be nice."

***

Within three years of dating, Tyson and Aubrie had become very close. They were in love, and one could see it in their eyes. Tyson knew Aubrie was the woman of his dreams, and he wanted to spend the rest of his life with her. He secretly planned a dinner with his parents and with the Murphys to propose. Aubrie had no idea what was going on.

Tyson and Aubrie walked into the elegant Italian restaurant in the West Loop of Chicago. "Aw, this is so nice, Tyson. You got your parents and my parents here. What's going on?" Aubrie said.

He responded, "You will see. This is a special day for us. Be patient, my dear."

"Okay."

All of Aubrie's closest friends were there, including Kendra. Tyson guided Aubrie to her chair and gently pulled it out for her as she sat between her parents. Tyson whispered to a waiter for some wine. After the waiter had presented the wine and filled all the glasses, Tyson cleared his throat and tapped his glass. "Excuse me. I want to thank everyone for coming tonight." He got up, walked toward Aubrie, and grabbed her delicate hand in his. "Stand up, my love."

"Okay, baby."

"From the first moment I laid eyes on you, I knew you were the one for me. I can talk to you about anything, you encourage me, and I love that about you." He reached into his pocket and pulled out a black velour ring box.

"Tyson, what are you doing?" Aubrie said as tears filled her eyes.

He got down on one knee and said, "Ms. Aubrie Murphy, the love of my life, would you honor me and make me the happiest man alive by marrying me?"

"Yes, yes!"

Everyone applauded, and the women wiped their tears of joy. Tyson and Aubrie embraced, whispering in each other's ears, "I love you so much."

Later, Aubrie and all of her girlfriends decided to go to her house to discuss the wedding plans. Kendra arrived last. All her closest friends were there: Debbie, Vanilla, and Zoe. For some reason, Kendra felt out of place, as if she should not even be there. She felt secluded because no one was talking to her about the plans. After being there for close to an hour, Kendra decided to leave. She didn't want to show disrespect to Aubrie, but she had other obligations that day.

"Hey, Aubrie, congratulations again. Let me know if you need help with any of the wedding plans. Sorry, but I have to go. I will call you later."

"Okay."

Six months has passed, and Tyson briefly spoke to Aubrie about his decision to join the United States Marine Corps. She was against it since there was a war in Iraq. The lovely couple started making their plans, but Tyson had to break some news to Aubrie.

"Tyson, I want a big, extravagant wedding!"

"Really, honey, we don't have the money," responded Tyson. "I was thinking of us going to city hall and maybe having an extravagant reception."

"What? Tyson, I don't like that idea."

"Well, Aubrie baby, there's a reason why, and you are not going to like it."

"Why? Tell me what's going on."

"Remember when I told you about my love for the armed forces?"

"Um, I think so."

"Well, we need to get married ASAP because I signed up for the Marine Corps. I ship out in six months."

"What! Tyson, I can't believe you! I thought that was just a childhood dream!"

"No! It's a vision. I have a great plan for our family. Just wait and see."

"Tyson, I don't want you going overseas to fight a senseless war! Are you crazy?"

"No. I will be fine. You have nothing to worry about, baby. We can write, call, email, and Skype. It will almost be like I'm in another state instead of another country."

"Wow, babe, it sounds like you've got it all together. It won't be the same with you not being here. I will miss you immensely."

"Babe, let's just spend as much time as possible together," said Tyson.

"That's all we can do, and you'd better come home to me as quickly as possible," responded Aubrie.

As both young ladies matured into adulthood, Kendra was growing and learning more about her relationship with God. In her adolescence, she'd struggled with depression and felt worthless, but through it all, God had been changing her, giving her peace within and unspeakable joy. She was taking a variety of classes, including one on rejection and how to deal with it and heal from it. She bought the book *God's Remedy for Rejection* by Derek Prince. Kendra knew this was a class she and Aubrie both needed, so she called and invited Aubrie to go with her. "Hey, Aubrie, my sista, how are you? What's going on?"

"I'm not your sista," responded Aubrie.

"Man, it's just a playful, cute term. What's wrong with that?"

"Like I said, we are friends, not sisters."

"Okay. How are you?"

"I'm good. Just working on my long-distance relationship with Tyson. It's hard, but I know since God brought us to it, he will bring us through it."

"Amen, Aubrie. I heard that. I know you have your own church, but I would like to invite you to one of my Sunday school classes. We are talking about rejection and how it can impact our lives."

Aubrie responded, "Oh, okay. What time does it start?"

"It starts at eight in the morning and ends at nine. So if you wanted to, you could come and then leave to go to your church or stay for the entire service."

"Okay, thanks, Kendra. I'll think about it."

"Well, that's the only reason I called. I will talk to you later. Let me know what you decide."

"Okay, will do," responded Aubrie.

A month passed, and Aubrie had not called or mentioned the rejection class. Kendra called to see what she'd been up to. "Hello, Aubrie. How are you?"

"I'm okay. How are you, Kendra?"

"I'm good. Thanks for asking. Aubrie, the rejection class is almost over. Do you think you will make it one Sunday morning?"

"Kendra, I don't know. You act like something is wrong with me. I'm fine."

"Okay, Aubrie, I hear you. I will not bother you with this again."

"Well, I gotta go, Kendra. Talk to you later."

"Okay, bye, Aubrie."

Kendra said to herself, "Wow, I guess she thinks I'm attacking her. All I can do is pray for her and the situation. Lord, it is now in your hands!"

More Drama, Jealousies, and Insecurities

Kendra had always enjoyed her friendships with other girls her age, especially since she desired to have a sister. She made an entry in her journal:

It is a known fact that women sometimes cannot get along with each other. Jealousies, envy, and competition usually break up or interfere; personality usually takes over. That's why some women say, "I don't have female friends. I prefer men. We get along better." Sometimes it might be that an individual does not like who you are as a person, and that's okay. Move on to a true friend. I think Kenny Rogers said it best: 'You've got to know when to fold 'em' and call it quits because some friendships are only for a season, and that's okay. You live and learn.

This was not Kendra's first encounter with having issues with women. She remembered her roommate from college, who'd been troubled and appeared to be a little crazy.

Tatiana Jacobson was a quiet young lady and a big-time loner. Sometimes she was friendly and talkative, and other times she was reserved, as if she hated every living being. It was almost as if she had more than one personality. She stood about five feet seven inches thin and frail. She looked ten years older than her age. Her clothes hung off her, not fitting her one bit. She could have passed for an anorexic. When Kendra had met her at school, she'd later learned of the trials and tribulations she'd experienced in life.

Tati was her nickname, and while she was away at George Washington University, her mother suddenly passed away. Those two women had had an awesome bond; they were like best friends. Everybody called them twins. After that day, Tati changed and looked at life and people differently. She lived with a closed mind and heart, not allowing anyone in.

Kendra and Tati lived in the same dorm and became friends the last quarter of their senior year. However, a couple of weeks before graduation, Kendra saw someone different in Tati. She gave Kendra the cold shoulder. She would get Kendra's attention only to belittle her and make her feel bad. Kendra learned that they both had attained jobs at the same Chicago publishing company.

One day Kendra was in the kitchen at work, preparing her coffee while talking and laughing with others, when Tati came in and mocked her. "Ha-ha-hee," she said with an attitude, and she left abruptly, almost bumping into Kendra.

"What's wrong with her?" said Shaquan, Kendra's coworker.

"Girl, I have no idea," responded Kendra.

It was a brand-new day, and Kendra was thrilled about her new position as a supervisor at the Chicago publishing company. She drove into her parking space as she continued to contemplate Tati and her attitude. "I don't know what's going on with Tati," Kendra whispered to herself. "Last month, she was cool, but as soon as I got my promotion, she started treating me as if I'm her enemy. I will pray for her. God will work it out. Some people will like you, and others will not, and that's okay, I guess. I just don't get it. What did I ever do to her to deserve such treatment? I'm gonna try to find out."

Just as Kendra entered the shiny black building, she saw Tati. "Good morning, Tati," Kendra said clearly, smiling, hoping Tati would acknowledge her this time.

"Hmm," she replied in a short and sharp manner, as if she were trying to start some mess. She looked around as if Kendra were Casper the friendly ghost.

"She's got a lot of nerve," Kendra whispered under her breath. "Hey, girl," Kendra said, waving to get her attention, and Tati leisurely turned her head the other way. "Wow! I don't even know anymore, but I'm gonna leave her alone for real this time."

Even though both ladies worked for the same department, Kendra made it her business to avoid Tati. One day Kendra was behind with her scheduling and had a late lunch. In the lunchroom that evening, she found Tati.

Kendra and Tati had been friends for a short time while working at the publishing company. They'd eaten lunch together, and then, suddenly, Tati had changed. Kendra kept her distance and even decided to eat lunch elsewhere.

Four months later, when the winter season set in, Kendra came back to the lunchroom, and Tati was there. When Tati saw Kendra, she looked at her with disdain, cocked her head, and smacked her lips, as if she were upset to see her. Kendra smiled and whispered to herself, "This is unbelievable. Is she still tripping? God bless her because there's nothing else I can do but pray for her. Oh my, so sad."

Kendra sat at the east end of the lunchroom, and Tati was on the west end. Within forty-five minutes, Kendra packed up her stuff and kept an eye on Tati, who had an insane habit of irritating Kendra by positioning herself to bump into her on purpose. Kendra slowly walked to the west doors, and Tati hurriedly grabbed her things, as if she were going to do something. Kendra stopped in her tracks. "Really?" She went back to her table, saw some coworkers, and said hi to stall Tati. She waited ten minutes and then proceeded to leave, and she was able to escape the crazy lady successfully.

Kendra decided to speak to other coworkers who knew Tati, and they agreed she was crazy. One minute she's your friend, and the next minute, she hated you. Kendra watched from afar how Tati associated with people in general. She was actually friendly. They would greet her and say hello, and she would respond. Kendra thought, *Maybe I should try one more time to talk to Tati*, but each time she came across her in the ladies' room, Tati always ignored Kendra. So Kendra was determined to return the favor. The more Kendra avoided her, the more Tati appeared to get in Kendra's space. Kendra came to the conclusion that Tati just did not like Kendra, and that was okay. Kendra said to herself, "I will continue to pray."

Aalia Grace was a sweet and positive woman. She was full-figured and comfortable in her skin. She'd struggled with her weight ever since she was a preteen. Aalia met Kendra at the Chicago publishing company; she was a temp in the editing department. One day they had lunch and began to talk about friendships with other women and how difficult those relationships could be.

"Kendra, I just want a friend or a sister I can connect with. I guess I want it so badly that I end up accepting the wrong people in my life."

"What do you mean, Aalia?"

"Well, I befriended a lady who worked with my sister. She appeared to be nice until I started losing weight. All of sudden, she started calling me a white girl."

"White girl? What is that supposed to mean?"

"She is much bigger than me, and she considers me to be skinny compared to her. Sounds silly, right?"

"Yeah. Evidently she has some insecurities about herself," said Kendra. "Aalia, you will always have a friend in me."

"Thanks, Kendra."

"But I know exactly what you are talking about when it comes to friendships with women." Kendra recognized that women in general seemed to have a problem with her, and she was having a hard time figuring out what was going on. *Is it because God is in the process of giving me freedom in him, like my Sunday school teacher said? I think so.*

As Kendra had more similar experiences, she slowly had a revelation: "I think most of these women have low self-esteem and are insecure, or maybe it's jealously!"

Kendra had left the supervisory position at the publishing company and started a new job at Metra, in the customer service department. She knew working with the public could be an adventure. However, sometimes coworkers could be just as bad. Kendra was working near Evanston when she encountered Dee Dee. She was an attractive lady, maybe in her midforties. There was never an official introduction between Kendra and Dee Dee, but Dee Dee had the nastiest attitude toward Kendra. Kendra thought to herself, *Oh my goodness, did she have a bad childhood, or is she in a horrible relationship, or does she just hate everyone?* Kendra discovered that Dee Dee had a problem with every woman she came in contact with, but only new women she didn't know. All of her other female coworkers she befriended were cool, but if one was a newbie, that girl could forget it.

The first day Kendra saw Dee Dee, Dee Dee was walking toward Kendra, and Kendra made eye contact and tried to smile and speak, but Dee Dee frowned and looked the other way. The interaction left a bad feeling with Kendra.

For lunchtime, Kendra always brought food that needed to be warmed, since Metra had a small lunchroom. One day Kendra was warming her food, when Dee Dee entered the tiny area. Dee Dee sighed as if Kendra were in her way. Kendra looked back and disregarded her, waiting for the microwave countdown. Dee said, "Excuse me," with an attitude.

"Okay," answered Kendra, allowing her to squeeze into the chair sitting in front of the microwave.

Bonnie, another coworker, interfered and said, "Oh, Dee Dee, don't let Kendra drop her hot food on you!"

Kendra thought to herself, *Oh my goodness, these women are so messy!* "Excuse me," Kendra said, carrying her food tray over Dee's head.

She gave Kendra a disgraceful look, as if to say, "If you drop any food on me, I will let you have it!"

Kendra thought to herself, *These women have a serious problem. Let me eat my food and get out of here!*

Men and women alike knew Dee Dee had issues. They would say things like "Oh, Dee Dee is a sweet person; don't mind her. That's just how she is."

Kendra wanted to ask someone, "Well, did she treat you like dirt when you first met her?"

Dee Dee was different with men; she was as sweet as pie, turning on her charm. She'd say to the janitor, Joey, "Hey, Joey, I brought you something back from my vacation. Let me go get it." But if a woman passed by her, she turned into an evil diva and became the angry black woman. Kendra did her best to avoid her at all cost. It was almost as if the only way Dee Dee knew to make a friend was through anger and conflict.

Sharing a Promotion after College

Kendra sensed something different about Aubrie; she felt more jealously and insecurity from her. Kendra was on her way to Bible study one day, when she received a call from Aubrie.

"Hey, Kendra, what's goin' on?"

"Oh, nothing. At church for Bible study. What's been up with you?"

"Girl, I'm trying to be patient waiting on Tyson to call me from Iraq. This is really difficult. I wish he would come home already."

"Yeah, I know. You gotta keep praying. God will work it all out. Speaking of working it out, guess what, Aubrie!"

"What?"

"I am so excited! I got a promotion at work, and it was so overdue. I am now the supervisor in the customer service department at Metra. I got a pay increase, and this is going to really help me financially. Isn't that great?"

Aubrie responded dryly, "Wow, that's great."

"I told my parents, and they are so proud of me. This couldn't be a better day. Aubrie, are you there?"

"Yeah, I'm here. Um, I gotta go. I will call you later, Kendra. I've got another call. I think it's from Tyson."

"Okay. Don't stop praying, Aubrie. All is well."

"Thanks. Bye," said Aubrie.

Kendra thought to herself, *Aubrie is changing, and I don't like it at all. Should I separate myself from her? What should I do to make this situation better? Lord, I really need your help.*

Aubrie Starts Comparing Herself to Others Again

As insecure Aubrie continued to compare herself to others, Aubrie and Kendra's friendship became more intense. Kylita, a friend Kendra had met in college, was cool. She was focused on school and her career and was extremely mature. She was someone Kendra needed as a friend. Kylita and Kendra made a pact. "Let's keep in touch," Kylita said.

"Okay," responded Kendra.

Over the years, the ladies were successful with their bond of staying connected.

As time went on, Kendra introduced all her friends to Aubrie. Everything appeared to be smooth until Kylita bought a townhouse.

"Aubrie, how are you?" Kendra said.

"I'm good, Kendra. What's up?"

"Oh, nothing. Remember my friend Kylita?"

"Yeah, what about her?"

"She just bought a house. Isn't that great?"

"Yeah, where is the house?"

"Near the northern suburbs of Chicago. Rosemont. She is having a housewarming party, and I wondered if you wanted to go with me."

"Hmm, naw, that's okay. She's probably gonna have a million people there that I won't know."

"So what, Aubrie? You know me. Plus, this is a great opportunity to make new friends. I can't believe you said that. I thought this would be a good experience for you since you are also looking to be a first-time homeowner. You can get tips on how she did her party."

"Naw, that's okay. Let me know what happens."

"Okay, I gotta go buy Kylita a gift. Talk to you later."

"All right, bye," said Aubrie.

The following weekend on the phone, Kendra said, "Hey, Aubrie, what's up? Tell me something new."

"Girl, we need to go shopping so I can prepare for my new home."

"Yeah, okay. Girl, you should have gone to the party. It was really nice—plenty of food and people."

"See? I told you. I would have been so uncomfortable."

"Aubrie, what's gotten into you? You are changing. What happened to the social butterfly I've grown to love? I guess your new name should be the dead butterfly."

"Kendra, I gotta go." Aubrie quickly hung up the phone.

"Uh-oh, did I say something wrong?" As Kendra sat in the kitchen, drinking her ginger tea, she shook her head, reflecting on their friendship. She remembered how bossy Aubrie could be and recalled a day she would never forget. Aubrie had taken her abilities to the hundredth power, and Kendra had taken it like an idiot without a backbone. They were out of college and decided to go shopping in the suburbs. Kendra drove, and Aubrie ordered her around as if she were her personal chauffeur. "Oh, Kendra, let's go to Macy's. Oh, then let's go to Denny's for lunch."

Every now and then, Aubrie would try to be sincere and say, "Kendra, is there any place you would like to shop?"

"Well, yeah, let's go to the jean store."

"Okay. Then after that, we can go to Bed, Bath, and Beyond. Wow! We are having so much fun, right?"

All Kendra could do was roll her eyes and pray the nightmare would end. Kendra thought to herself, *What's wrong with you, Kendra? Are you afraid of standing up to Aubrie? Is she testing me?* Apparently, but as the years flew by, their attitude toward the friendship changed, and the distance and static grew between them. Before they knew it, a shift came, and Kendra was brand new with a mind of her own.

Tyson Gets Injured

Four years passed, and Tyson was suddenly injured. He would be coming home soon for good. Aubrie called Kendra with the bad news. Aubrie sat on her couch with her legs crossed, wiping her tears as she dialed Kendra's number. "Hey, Kendra, I need you to come over here right now."

"Why? What happened?"

"It's Tyson."

"Okay, hold on. I'm on my way."

As Kendra rode up the elevator six floors to Aubrie's apartment, she wondered what could possibly have happened to Tyson. "I hope he's okay, alive, and well. Lord, let Tyson be okay for Aubrie's sake." Kendra knocked on the door, unprepared for the mysterious news.

Aubrie opened the door, and Kendra walked in and said, "Aubrie, is everything okay? What happened?"

"Kendra, let's sit down."

"Okay."

"The marines called me early this morning at two o'clock. It frightened me, and I could not stop shaking. I thought the worst: *Tyson is dead*. But he was badly injured. He lost his left arm."

"What! Is he okay? How are you doing?"

"All I could do was cry and praise and thank God that he is alive. He has to heal and do therapy for six months, and then he will be home soon. I had to share this with somebody."

"Well, thank God for that. If you need me, I'm here. If you need anything, let me know, okay?"

"Kendra, can I have a hug?"

"Sure."

The ladies tightly embraced and wiped their tears.

***

Eight months passed, and Kendra hardly talked to or hung out with Aubrie. Kendra and Aubrie decided to do dinner and catch up since they had not spoken. The ladies met at a small sandwich shop in the West Loop. The women arrived in the parking lot, waving at one another. They entered the shop together.

"Hey, Aubrie, how are you?" Kendra said.

"I'm good. How are you, Kendra?"

"I'm all right. Aubrie, every time we meet, I notice you look at me in a funny way. Why are you looking at me that way? It's like I have something that you want."

Aubrie said, "I don't know. You have grown so much, and I feel like I'm stuck, not progressing or anything. It seems like you have it all together. Kendra, do you ever compare yourself to others?"

"Yeah, sometimes, but that can be dangerous, and it can get you in trouble. I am learning to celebrate others because sooner or later, the Lord can and will bless me in the same way. I know it's hard, but you have to take the focus off yourself and concentrate on God. And believe me, none of us has it together. That's why we have to trust and depend on God for everything. Aubrie, relax. You have been a wonderful wife, taking care of your husband. Take it easy, girl. Maybe you should get away and take some time for yourself. If you don't take care of yourself, who will? It's so easy to compare yourself to others, and the Enemy wants you to stay there and be miserable. We have to remember to renew our minds and try to avoid negative thinking. Aubrie, you need an attitude adjustment. I'm not trying to talk about you; I'm trying to help. If you talk to God about it, I am sure he will give you peace and understanding."

The Jealousy Is Real: Journeying beyond Jealousy

Kendra continued to go to her Sunday school class. She was growing tremendously. The teacher always encouraged the class to participate, so she decided to give each person a topic to speak on. Kendra's discussion piece was "Journeying beyond Jealousy." *Wow, right up my alley since there has been a very long conflict with Aubrie's and my friendship*, she thought.

Kendra hated to make presentations in front of people. She got extremely nervous. Every bone in her body vibrated with great intensity. She grew warm all over and could feel her armpits sweating. She thought to herself, *I hope my deodorant works today*. But she knew she could do the presentation successfully. She just wanted to get the ordeal over with, so she volunteered to go first.

"Good morning. My presentation is called 'Journeying beyond Jealousy,' and I can relate to this because I have had a great bond with my girlfriend since grammar school, but now as adults, we are growing further apart. I believe the conflict is jealousy. I have always loved singing and decided to join the choir, which kept me busy like a bumblebee. Each time my friend called to hang out, I was on the go with the choir. I did my best to make room for her, but it just didn't work. As I continued to grow as a singer, she started to look at me differently, with her head cocked to the side. It was like she was saying, 'I don't want to be your friend anymore.' Time after time, we would meet to discuss what the problem was, but the real truth was never exposed. We decided to go our own way with other friends who made us feel comfortable. All I can do is pray, give it over to God, and hope good change would come. Thank you."

Since Kendra had heard about Tyson and his injuries, she always made it her business to check on Aubrie and her husband to see how they were progressing. She picked up her phone one day and dialed Aubrie's number. "Hey, how is Tyson doing? How is he making the adjustment to having one arm?"

"Girl, it is very hard. We discussed him getting a prosthesis; however, they are very expensive."

"How expensive?"

"Between six thousand and eight thousand dollars."

"Wow! That's crazy."

"Plus, this cost usually has to be paid every three to four years due to wear and tear."

"What about medical insurance?"

"Most private plans have a cap on coverage for prosthetics, usually in the range of twenty-five hundred to five thousand dollars a year. And most insurance plans have some restrictions for cost on prosthetic care."

"That's a shame. With so many military people and others facing trauma to their bodies, more should be done."

"Yeah, and the politicians are not agreeing on passing a new law for prosthesis coverage for amputees. So until that happens or we do more research, Tyson is choosing to be without."

"Man, that's a lot to deal with."

"Yeah, we're gonna be okay."

"Yeah, I can't imagine being in your shoes. You have to think positively. Talk to you later."

Twenty Years Later

Twenty years passed, and Kendra and Aubrie remained friends. Kendra couldn't figure out how the friendship had continued for so long, since their likes had become so different. Every time Aubrie felt she was being treated unfairly, she would call Kendra and set up a café conversation. The conversation always seemed to go back to six months or a year ago, centering on old stuff neither one of them had had the guts to speak on at the time.

Kendra sat in her car, thinking, *What did I do this time for a meeting to be held? Whatever happens and whatever we discuss, I am going to be honest with myself and Aubrie.* Since Kendra had arrived slightly early, she decided to study her Bible because she knew Aubrie would be late. "Let me look at Proverbs chapter seventeen in the Good News Bible. Wow, verse nine is speaking to me right now: 'If you want people to like you, forgive them when they wrong you. Remembering wrongs can break up a friendship.' That is exactly what is happening with Aubrie and me. We recall very old issues and accuse one another. It's almost like we have horrible communication skills. We talk about it, but no truths are discussed, and nothing is resolved." Kendra thought to herself, *It's amazing to me how she wants to talk and communicate but is not being truthful with herself. What is there to discuss if you are not being truthful? Lord, help me get an understanding of this!*

Kendra could never say what was on her mind. When something would bother her, she would rehearse it repeatedly. "Okay, here we go," she said to herself. "Listen, Aubrie, we've been friends for years, and lately, you haven't been yourself. Is there something going on or that you want to share with me?"

Kendra saw Aubrie, got out of her car, and greeted Aubrie at the restaurant doors. "Hey, Aubrie, you look nice today."

"Thank you."

They found a window booth seat. Kendra sensed an attitude with Aubrie. *Uh-oh, what is wrong with her now?* "Aubrie, what's going on with our friendship? Are you angry with me? Do you need to share some information with me? What's up?"

"What do you mean? I'm fine. I'm trying to figure out why we are here again for the twentieth time."

"What?" responded Kendra. "Are you crazy? This was your idea!"

"Okay, Kendra, I do have a confession."

"What is it?"

"Well, I was upset with you after Tyson proposed to me."

"Why? What did I do?"

"Remember when all the ladies met back at my house to hang and talk? We did not finish the discussion about my wedding plans, and it was like you did not care, or you were not interested. You left, remember?" Aubrie sighed and rolled her eyes.

"You should not take that to heart. I told you I had something to do. Plus, to me, nothing was being discussed anyway. I'm sorry if I hurt your feelings."

"That's okay."

"Well, speaking of hurt feelings, I feel like you are not my friend anymore, or you don't even like me as a person."

"What do you mean?"

"Something happened between us, and it's like it's a dark secret. What's goin' on?"

"I don't know, Kendra. Maybe we should slowly try to talk more often than we do now."

"So if we do that, how often should we contact one another? Aubrie, how about monthly?"

"Okay. It's worth a try."

Within a month, Kendra forgot their plan. Aubrie called and was furious. "Hey, Kendra, I thought we were going to touch base every month?"

"Aubrie, it's not working. Every time we talk, there's nothing to talk about. The last time, we just sat on the phone mostly in silence."

"Kendra, that's a start. Don't you think that's better than nothing?"

"I guess so."

"Kendra, since you aren't talking about anything, I will talk to you later."

"Okay."

Once again their plan to fix the friendship failed.

Kendra wanted to drop the so-called friendship. It was draining her, and they weren't accomplishing anything, but for some reason, they both continued to hold on to it. A month later, Aubrie and Kendra went to visit Tyson as he recovered from his injuries. He found out about Kendra's singing career and that she was working on a CD. Aubrie let Tyson listen to a few singles.

"Kendra, congratulations on that single 'Love Is. ' It's wonderful, and I love it. Keep it up. I can see you doing big things," Tyson said.

"Really, Tyson?"

"Yes."

"Thanks, man." Kendra glanced at Aubrie, who had a distasteful look on her face, as if she did not want her husband to congratulate Kendra on being successful. "Wow," whispered Kendra, "maybe it's time for me to walk away from this friendship. Too much tension and craziness. I can do without this."

As Kendra thought back on the past, she had an aha moment. Aubrie sometimes appeared to be jealous or irritated at Kendra's social network, which wasn't much in Kendra's eyes. They were friends, and Kendra would always invite Aubrie to hang out at single or young-adult events or walkathons. One time, there was a movie night, and both young ladies attended. While they were in line to get refreshments, Aubrie asked a question, and Kendra thought she answered her nicely, but Aubrie said, "Every time I come to church with you, you are mean to me!"

Shocked, Kendra said, "What! I am not mean, and if you think so, I'm sorry."

It was always something that bothered her. Kendra thought attending different events at church would help Aubrie make a decision on choosing a church home, but Kendra later found out they would not be attending the same church, and that was best.

They never analyzed their disagreements to see what was really going on with each person. They never thought to dig deeper; they'd just walk away and go forward until the next episode. Kendra later learned in her rejection class that some people were easily offended; they had offended spirits. Nothing anyone did or did not do could help the situation. The offended person was extremely sensitive, and his or her feelings got hurt easily. How could a person like that have healthy friendships or relationships in general?

What Happened to the Friendship?
Is Aubrie Having A Midlife Crisis?

As April approached, the ladies came together again to try to celebrate Kendra's birthday by having dinner at a restaurant. During dinner, the conversation turned to being truthful with one's friends. Kendra usually took the easy path. She would avoid confrontation, and if that meant being dishonest, so be it.

"Kendra, does my breath stink?" Aubrie asked.

"No, why do you ask?"

"I've been having problems with my teeth, and it feels like my breath stinks most of the time. Does it?"

"I don't know, maybe," responded Kendra.

"Maybe? Kendra, the answer is yes or no." Aubrie was becoming irritated by Kendra's uncertainty.

"Um, a little bit, I guess."

Aubrie exploded with anger. "Kendra, how come you didn't tell me the first time? See? This is what I'm talking about. We are supposed to be the best of friends, and you can't even tell me if my breath stinks. Maybe this friendship needs to be reviewed to see what is really going on."

Kendra frowned and said, "Girl, it's not that serious!"

"Well, it's serious to me. Are you done eating? Because I'm ready to go."

"No, I need a carryout container."

"Girl, you can't finish that?"

"No, I'm full, and I don't want to stuff myself."

The waiter brought Kendra her container, and they left the restaurant. During the ride home, one could have heard a pin drop. Kendra felt uneasy and was afraid to say anything to Aubrie. Aubrie was heated, and Kendra could not understand why.

The ladies continued to spend less and less time together. They did not speak to each other for more than three months. Then they bumped into each other at the lakefront.

Kendra looked ahead as she held hands with her boyfriend, Xavier. She thought to herself, *Uh-oh, that looks like Aubrie and Tyson.*

"Well, Kendra, it's been a minute since we've talked. What have you been up to, and who is this guy? Is he your man?" Aubrie said.

"Aubrie, it has been a long time. This is my boyfriend, Xavier. Xavier, this is Aubrie and Tyson."

Tyson said, "Wow, that's great. I am really happy for you both."

"Thanks, Tyson." After the compliment, Kendra noticed Aubrie. Her face looked blank, as if she was shocked Kendra had a man in her life. Then, all of a sudden, she gave a wide smile, as if someone had a gun to her head and was forcing her to smile.

After they said their goodbyes and walked away, Kendra whispered to Xavier, "Wow, what was that? She's not really happy for me, and it's a shame she can't be honest with me and herself! Did you see how she was looking at me—at us?"

"Kendra, I don't know what you are talking about. I don't see why you guys still consider yourselves to be friends with so much negativity going back and forth."

"I guess you are right, but I really don't know what to do."

After Kendra arrived home, she couldn't shake what had happened earlier. Kendra's thoughts continued to flow as she thought about her friendship with Aubrie. "I don't know what happened to our friendship over the years."

Kendra remembered one of their last social events: an India Arie concert. Kendra's phone rang at the concert, so of course, she answered it. Later on, nosy Aubrie said, "Who was that?"

"Just Kylita."

"What did she want?"

"Oh, nothing. She was just saying hello."

Aubrie sighed and whispered, "Whatever."

Kendra ignored her. Kendra made it her business to make the friendship work, so two weeks later, she called Aubrie to see what her plans were for Labor Day. "Hello, Aubrie. How are you? What are your plans for Labor Day?"

"Hey, Kendra, I'm actually on my way to the Aurora Mall."

"Really? By yourself?"

"Naw, girl, I have a coworker with me."

Kendra was kind of shocked. That information stung, but she shook it off. "Oh, okay. I'll let you go so you can concentrate on driving."

"Kendra, I will call you back and tell you about all the deals I found. Maybe you can come over too so we can hang out."

"Okay, let me know."

They both were making new friends, growing, and maturing into hardworking professional women. As things changed, both ladies experienced platonic jealousy. They both feared being replaced and competing with or being compared to someone else. When Thanksgiving and Christmas came around, they often had dinner at each other's house, but not every year. Aubrie was materialistic and a shopaholic. There was a void in her life, and she was trying to fill it with things. The ladies would always have the same conversation about Christmas. Every time Kendra turned around, Aubrie was negative about anything Kendra did.

"So, Kendra, are you doing any Christmas shopping this year?"

"No, we do it at work, but I just don't have the money."

"What do you mean?"

"Well, my supervisor loves the holidays, so out of the goodness of her big heart, she buys gifts for all her employees. She is super nice."

"Do you ever buy her a gift?"

"No. Like I said, I can't afford it. I wish I could, but I can't right now. I need to start adding to my budget in advance."

"Man, that's not right. If people buy me a gift I did not expect, I go buy them a gift even if I don't like them."

"Now, that's crazy, and you are not being real to me, Aubrie. How does the saying go? 'It is better to give than to receive.' People should not be giving in order to receive. If that's the case, a person will be very upset with me because I'm real. You give me a gift, and I will give you a thank-you in return. But let's say a person gives me a discount on my hairstyle, or someone does something nice for me. In instances like that, I will give back if I know your heart. I give to those I feel deserve it and have the right attitude. We were talking about this in my Sunday school class. I read, 'Everything about giving reflects the grace of God. We should not be giving as a sense of legal requirement or mere duty or compulsion. Giving should be joyful, not forced, you know.'"

"Well, I disagree. I feel bad when that happens. Speaking of gifts, I have one for you this Christmas, Kendra."

"Oh, okay. Thanks."

Aubrie handed her a white envelope, and Kendra opened it. Inside was a twenty-dollar gift certificate to Macy's.

"Thanks, Aubrie. That was very thoughtful of you."

When Kendra went home, she vented to her mom. "Mom, why would a person give a gift like that? Aubrie has always said she doesn't like it when people give her gift certificates, but she gives one to me? I don't know anymore. I guess I should be thankful regardless, but I don't know if she was trying to be funny. I can never tell you where that girl's mind is at times."

Friendship and Communication

Kendra made sure she kept a journal of what was going on in their so-called friendship.

Communication is key. Real, true friends are honest about everything, I think. They don't worry about hurting your feelings. They tell you how they feel that moment. They keep it real—100 percent real talk.

"It's a year later, and oh, by the way, that thing you did hurt me!"

"How come you didn't tell me?"

"I don't know. You know I don't like confrontation."

And who does? There are some who like to argue and debate. That ain't me. Let's speak calmly and openly. Some people are afraid of the truth. They just lie and enjoy living it. My pastor said it best: "They live the lie so long that they start to enjoy it." Sometimes you can confront people, and they will lie to your face. What a shame! That's Aubrie. She has a lot of pride, and it keeps her from admitting her faults. This experience will help me to be a better friend to the next one and to the friends I have. I hope each person reflects on what went wrong. How did each person contribute? What could have been done differently to have a happier ending or for the friendship to end and not hold on to something that would never be?

Aubrie looked up to Kendra, but somehow, her response turned to envy and jealousy. When they reunited after college, both young ladies attended their own church. Kendra was more committed and would not allow anything to stop her from attending. For example, Kendra had a car accident that totaled her car, so she had to use public transportation from the northwest side and then travel southeast for church. Kendra found a way, and she was okay with it.

As Aubrie was finishing her bachelor's degree at Roosevelt University, Kendra joined her to complete her master's. Aubrie commented on the situation. One day during midterms, Aubrie saw Kendra reading in the dining hall, so she decided to stop by. "Hey, Kendra, how are you? What's up?"

"Hey, Aubrie. Trying to prepare for my English midterm. I gotta hurry 'cause I want to do Bible study tonight."

"Oh, girl, you are good. If it was up to me, I would stay home."

"No, Aubrie, I need all the help I can get to pass these midterms, and going to Bible study helps me focus more and depend on God."

"Oh, really? I was just thinking about not going to church Sunday because I need to get my hair done. I hate to go to church with a nappy head!"

"Aubrie, I understand. We all have bad hair days or days when we just don't feel like doing anything, but you should not allow your hair to be an excuse not to go to church. If you don't want to go or don't feel like it, don't go. And please don't blame it on the condition of your hair, Aubrie!"

"Oh well, Kendra. I don't see how you do it. If it was me, I would not go to church on the bus. I've been extremely spoiled and need my car to travel, especially in the wintertime. Girl, you are good! I don't want to interrupt your studying, so I will talk to you later."

"Okay," said Kendra.

Aubrie and Kendra spent less and less time together. It was almost as if Aubrie was pushing Kendra away. Their conversations on the phone came to a halt. Instead of calling Kendra, Aubrie started texting her, and that made matters worse. Aubrie realized Kendra had gone on with her life with other friends, and that bothered her, but she did not bring it up in conversation. Was Aubrie embarrassed to admit she was jealous and feeling rejected? How did Kendra deal with those feelings? She ignored them and decided to hang out with other friends from her church. Aubrie and Kendra had done everything together, maybe even too much, so as they got older, maybe they just got tired of one another. As Kendra went her own way and the Lord placed new people in her life, she realized friendship did not necessarily mean talking every day and doing everything together.

Kendra was maturing and realizing a person could have a variety of friends at different levels. As Kendra got more involved in church, God changed, healed, and delivered her. Aubrie saw the change, and it did not sit well with her. It was as if their friendship were a game, and Aubrie had to compete for something, which made no sense to Kendra. She just wanted some harmony in their friendship and did not know how to achieve it. One of her spiritual mothers shared with her a message: "Girl, when God gives you freedom in him, the people around you start looking at you funny."

Aubrie was raised in the church, and Kendra was not. As the years sped by, the situation flipped. Kendra slowly developed a relationship with God, and Aubrie stopped in her tracks as she searched for a new church home. No one knew why this occurred. After a while, Aubrie got back in church, but in her mind, from her perspective, church was a competition with Kendra. One day, while they were driving in the car, Aubrie shared one of her experiences with Kendra. "Girl, let me tell you what happened to me recently! I got the Holy Ghost, and a prophet spoke about my future. What do you think about that?"

Kendra said, "That's good, Aubrie. Why are you telling me? You act like you are trying to prove a point. That's private and doesn't need to necessarily be shared with everyone."

"Well, I thought it needed to be shared with you because you are my friend. By the way, when are you coming to church with me? It is so different from your church. The saints are so welcoming and loving."

"Aubrie, whenever you want me to, just let me know." Kendra thought to herself, *Is she dissing my church? What is wrong with her? I really don't feel like debating with her. I am going to let this slide. Jesus, you are going to have to help me.*

The Revelation

After Kendra realized Aubrie really wasn't her friend anymore, Kendra started to focus on Aubrie's behavior. Kendra knew Aubrie had downcast moments when she felt depressed. The depression would cause her not to go to church for long periods of time.

"Hey, Aubrie, how are you?" Kendra asked one day.

"I'm okay. I guess I'm sad because Tyson lost his arm. Sometimes it's hard for me to be strong for him."

"Aubrie, I know it's been difficult. That's why I'm calling. Do you plan on going to church Sunday?"

"I don't know. Why?"

"I would like to go to church with you. You need your spirit lifted, and you need to hear the Word."

"Kendra, you are right."

"So are you going, Aubrie?"

"Yeah, Kendra, meet me at my house at nine thirty tomorrow morning. We can go to the first service."

"Okay, cool. I will see you tomorrow."

Kendra decided to wear a patterned sundress that was brown, navy, and green. She thought she looked nice. When Kendra looked good and especially felt good, Aubrie knew how to try to make her feel bad. Kendra knocked on the door.

"Hey, Kendra."

"Hey, Aubrie."

Aubrie looked Kendra up and down silently and then said, "That's an interesting dress you're wearing."

Kendra considered that a compliment and said, "Thank you."

"Come on, Kendra. Let's go."

They got in the elevator and rode down three floors. The elevator doors opened, and they walked to the exit doors and to Aubrie's car. They arrived at the church parking lot and found a good spot. They got out of the car and followed the other anxious, joyful saints. Kendra caught a guy's eye, but he shook his head as if he did not approve of her appearance. At the time, Kendra was transitioning with her hair, so she wore a wig. Aubrie noticed as well and chuckled out loud. Kendra took a deep breath and tried to erase the situation from her mind. Kendra thought to herself, *What was that? Is Aubrie happy about what just happened? Was she laughing at me? Friends don't do that. That hurt.*

Once the ladies entered the church, they saw a lot of young people there from twenty-five to forty. Kendra caught the eye of one fellow. He appeared to be much younger. He stared at her, and she gazed back. Aubrie watched from afar and sighed under her breath. Kendra said to herself, *Do I sense some jealousy? I think it's true! This is starting to stress me out. I don't think I can take it. What should I do?*

After talking with her Sunday school teacher, Kendra realized she had a problem. She always found herself doing things to please others, even though it made her feel uncomfortable. She needed to stop the disease to please others and start doing things to please God and herself. Kendra thought to herself, *Maybe I can't put all the blame on Aubrie. I guess I have played a part in the downfall of this friendship.*

Pursuing Dreams

After Kendra graduated from college, there was a talent show sponsored by *Soul Train*, the American musical variety show. The first- and second-place winners would appear on the show as special guests. Johanna Golden was an older woman of God. She was African American and was plus-sized but fierce, and she called herself superficial. She at least had to have color on her lips, if not her entire face made up. She always had to look presentable. She would question Kendra, saying, "Where are your lipstick and mascara?"

"I have lipstick on. You don't see it?"

"No."

Kendra explained, "I don't like wearing mascara. It gives me raccoon eyes."

"Oh, okay. But you need to add some color to those pretty brown eyes and make them pop."

"Okay."

Johanna was wise beyond her years but had a great sense of humor and made life fun in every way. Kendra met Johanna at the talent show, where Johanna was a contestant also. Kendra had to finish her makeup and highlight her gorgeous, big brown eyes.

As Kendra and Aubrie entered the ladies' room, they saw and heard Johanna. "Do, re, mi, fa, so, la, ti, do!"

"Oops! Sorry, ma'am. We didn't mean to interrupt you," said Kendra.

"Girl, please don't worry about it," responded Johanna. "Are you singing in the competition?"

"Yes, how did you know?"

"All singers have a look, and, girl, you've got that look!"

"Oh, okay. Thanks, I guess," said Kendra.

Aubrie frowned, not agreeing with the conversation. She backed away, as if she did not belong, and became quiet.

Johanna said, "By the way, I'm Johanna. What's your name?"

"I'm Kendra, and my friend Aubrie has suddenly disappeared. Where did that girl go?"

Johanna responded, "Hmm. I know you don't know me, but that girl is not your friend. I can tell by her actions, and I can sense it."

"What? What do you mean? We have been friends since fourth grade."

"Kendra, I'm telling you—she's not your friend. If you have not seen the signs, you will eventually. Good luck."

Kendra did not know how to respond to that horrible information. She could only pray and pay attention, as Johanna had said. *Now all of this craziness I've been going through is making sense*, Kendra thought to herself.

The talent show was off the chain. Kendra surprised herself—she won first place. Johanna placed second. Kendra and Johanna exchanged numbers and became good friends. Johanna was like a big sister to Kendra. As the ladies got to know one another, they discovered they were April babies, so they got along well. Johanna was just what Kendra needed—a sister to teach, advise, and mentor her regarding dating, careers, prayer, and life in general. Johanna taught Kendra the importance of prayer and being detailed in telling God exactly what you needed.

"Johanna, I don't know what I'm going to do since my car accident. I really need an inexpensive car with no car note," Kendra said one day.

"Did you tell God what you wanted?"

"Yeah."

"Well, I think it's time for us to come in agreement through pray with you, and we will continue until you find the car you are looking for."

"Okay."

They prayed Monday through Friday, day in and day out, not skipping a beat, usually at four in the morning. After about two months of prayer, Kendra was able to purchase a 2005 Toyota Avalon with a sunroof and CD player, and even though she had a note, it was only $200 a month because of her decent credit.

"See, Kendra? Ain't God good?" Johanna said.

"Yes, he is."

"Now we need to focus on your love life. You want to be married, right?"

"I sure do."

"Write all the qualities you want in a man, and please be specific."

"Okay."

All of a sudden, Kendra met a new man almost every week. She met a guy she worked with and dated him, but it didn't work out. Right after she broke up with him, she said, "No more dating, just friendship." But she'd spoken too soon because immediately thereafter, she met a new guy, John. After a year and a half, they were still together and planned on marrying in a couple of years.

Kendra analyzed everything Aubrie did, and she finally started to believe what her mom and Johanna told her. Aubrie and Kendra spoke less and less. Aubrie had no idea Kendra had a love life, and Kendra was going to keep it that way. That type of situation happened more than once, and Kendra didn't question it. She just made a mental note. Since Aubrie and Kendra's friendship was falling apart, Kendra did not know what to do. She tried her best to make the relationship work.

During that time, she met another older woman who was a mentor to her. The woman was old enough to be her mother but turned out to be a great friend to Kendra. Willie Mae Rodriguez was from Puerto Rico. She had three sons and one grandson. She'd failed at marriage twice, but after becoming a Christian, she said she would be willing to try one more time. She was a romantic at heart. Kendra met Willie Mae at Metra. They became lunch buddies. During their lunch breaks, Willie Mae shared testimonies of her life, including things she'd learned the hard way. "Kendra, when I was your age, I loved to party and dance. That's all I did. I also enjoyed dating. I've had some of the most horrible relationships. I dealt with abusive men, and I had to get out. I also had a very active sex life. I just want to tell you that it is best for you to wait for marriage if you can. Don't give your cookies away too soon or to any Joe Blow. You hear me?"

"Yes," Kendra replied. "Willie Mae, can I ask you a question?"

"Sure."

"I have a friend I've known since grammar school, and lately, there has been so much tension. I actually feel better when I hang out with other friends. She continues to compare herself to me. One day she told me, 'Kendra, I find myself being jealous of others who are doing well in life. I know that's not right. I don't know why I feel this way.' Willie Mae, I didn't know how to respond to that."

"Well, Kendra, there is something going on with her, and she needs to talk to God about it and dig deep. It sounds like she might be an insecure person."

"Really?"

"Yep. Just continue to pray for your friend."

"Yeah, I do, but sometimes it's hard."

As Kendra continued to groom her singing career, she performed at several events. There was one in particular she would not forget: a singing competition in Hyde Park. The winner would get two first-class tickets to *The Ellen DeGeneres Show* and perform live. As Kendra walked around backstage, she noticed a lady giving her the evil eye. She was a singer too. She continued staring at Kendra as if to say, "I'm gonna win this competition. You don't have a chance."

Once again, Kendra thought, *How come women cannot compete in a nice way without getting ugly? I just don't get it!*

Kendra did her best to ignore that situation. She focused on her performance and won the competition.

Thought of Abandonment

As Kendra thought to herself, she wrote in her journal,

> Maybe I've abandoned Aubrie, but I think she has abandoned me too as a friend. Our thoughts and emotions have changed over the years. Neither of us can change or force one another to think or act a certain way, and with that being said, it is best to abandon the friendship, in my eyes. God is in control!

Aubrie planned on having a huge celebration for her forty-first birthday, and everyone knew about it, including Kendra. Her birthday was August 1, and she decided to invite all her friends whose birthdays were in August. When Kendra heard about the party, she looked forward to going but wasn't sure if she would attend. She was torn. She listened to her intuition, reviewed her friendship, and acknowledged that her friendship with Aubrie should have ended years ago. Why had Kendra hung on for so long, and if Aubrie felt the same way, why did she hang on?

The friendship slowly faded away. There was no talking or hanging out. They both could sense a weird, unfriendly, tense vibe. It was over. There was no more drama or craziness. Kendra was finally honest with herself and free. She walked away with no explanation.

After walking away, the ladies somewhat kept in touch every year for their birthdays. They would share one phone call, and that was it until the next year. It was difficult for them to let go after being friends for more than twenty-five years. Kendra tried to make sense of the situation by sharing her story with others. Kendra was talking to a coworker named Nina one day, saying she could not believe how unfriendly people at work could be by not saying good morning.

"You know what I do, Kendra? I decided to walk by and not say a thing. Why would a person look directly in your face and not say good morning? I look at them like they are crazy. I give them what they give out.!"

"Yeah, I understand exactly," responded Kendra. "I had a good friend I've known since the fourth grade, and I knew we would be friends forever. At least I thought I did, until she started changing and acting as if I were her enemy. I would be driving and see her car approaching me, and I know we both made eye contact, but guess what."

"What, Kendra?"

"She'd turn her head as if she didn't see me. What was that? What do you call that?"

"I don't know, girl," responded her coworker.

"But guess what I decided to do."

"What's that?"

"Not call. I just dropped and dismissed her, and she has no clue what's going on. A couple of years later, we saw one another, and this time, she looked so interested in trying to make eye contact. I acted like I didn't see her. Isn't that amazing?"

"Yep, girl, it's a trip."

"If we are friends, what would make her do that?"

"I don't know. Did you guys have a disagreement?"

"Not that I know of. All I know is, if she wants to act crazy, I can be a little bit crazier. You know, don't play with me!"

"Girl, I hear you, Kendra!"

Kendra reflected in her journal:

> We have been friends it seems like forever; however, Aubrie's actions made it seem as if she was not in my corner. The conflict really boils down to

insecurities. If you don't like or love yourself, how can you love or encourage someone else you consider to be a friend?

Kendra agreed with this thought process, but along the way, she'd learned that before this could happen, one had to get to the root of the problem. What happened? What caused the feelings and attitudes to change? Kendra had to ask herself, *Is the relationship worth the conflict or not?* She thought, *No!* because the conflict was continuous, even after they tried to discuss issues or problems. They never reviewed the real truth, and that was the reality of it. Aubrie just wanted to pretend as if nothing had happened and go on in her life. Kendra thought to herself, *Are we both guilty of holding grudges? Maybe.* Kendra believed something had happened in the friendship that had made Aubrie extremely angry, but she did not want to bring it up in a discussion to resolve the issue. Some people had totally different attitudes toward friendships. Some women became fed up with befriending other women.

Esther, Kendra's associate, explained it to her like this: "I don't have friends; I have associates. To avoid all the drama that comes with so-called friends, I call them my associates and chitchat for a minute, and that's it—no more, no less. When I call friends to chitchat, if they don't answer the phone, I don't leave a message either. They know how to get back in touch with me. There is no commitment of 'She'd better call me back.' We will talk. When we talk, there's no pressure here, and that's okay."

Kendra said, "In my friendship with Aubrie, she was so jealous of my gift of singing and other things, such as the attention my gift gave me, so when she came around with other friends, she completely ignored me. Who does that? Does she even realize that she is doing this?"

Kendra reflected as she wrote in her journal,

> Aubrie and I both had a revelation regarding the conflict and differences between us. We've matured since our college years. I was very angry with Aubrie at one time. But I had to forgive her and let it go. Initially, I was going to be done completely. When I really look at our friendship as a whole, it was difficult. I think we both matured and realized that we are friends but not like when we were ten years old. Too much time has passed. Now we talk periodically during special events or birthdays, and that's okay, and I guess that's how it will be from now on.

Kendra had thought their friendship could go the distance, but sadly, it had ended.

There were two women who exuded true, real friendship: Alice Albany and Etta Hemingway. They met at work when they were in their early twenties. Over a forty-year period, they both wed and vacationed together. A year ago, Mrs. Hemingway's husband died. During that time, Alice became a soldier on the battlefield on behalf of Etta. She was there at every turn, calling, visiting, and getting Etta out of the house. Whatever needed to be done, she did it. She did not wait or ask. Alice stepped up as a dear friend to Etta. That was the kind of friendship Kendra had longed for with Aubrie, but their friendship had turned out to be a little different.

As you can see, friendship can go either way. There may be ups and downs. It's possible for a friendship to have no major problems if the ladies have great true communication between each other and share all issues. On the other hand, a friendship can be like Aubrie and Kendra's. It started out great, but as time moved on, they both changed. When people change, they may not like each other anymore, and then issues are not truly discussed. To have a real, true friend is a blessing. Just remember, sometimes we may have to learn how to be a good friend or a better one in the future. At some point in life, we all have dreams, whether to have a successful career or to grow old with a friend. Just be careful because that dream may not come true, and that's okay. God may have a better plan for you.

Joyce Meyer Ministries made a profound statement about friendship: "True friends don't try to control you—they help you be what God wants you to be. Put your faith in God and ask Him to give you FRIENDS who are truly right for you!"

Questions

1. What do you think were the reasons Aubrie and Kendra's friendship fell apart?
2. Do you think women in general are hard to get along with? Why or why not?
3. Do you think Aubrie and Kendra were to blame for their failed relationship? Why or why not?
4. Do you think their friendship could have been saved and restored? How?
5. Have you ever had a difficult friendship? What happened, how did you handle it, and what were the results?
6. Who do you think you are more like: Kendra or Aubrie? Why?

Printed in the United States
By Bookmasters